HENRY HECKELBECK

Makes Super Slime

By **Wanda Coven**

Illustrated by **Priscilla Burris**

LITTLE SIMON

New York London Toronto Sydney New Delhi

LITTLE SIMON
An imprint of Simon & Schuster Children's Publishing Division
1230 Avenue of the Americas, New York, New York 10020
First Little Simon paperback edition December 2023
Copyright © 2023 by Simon & Schuster, LLC
Also available in a Little Simon hardcover edition.
All rights reserved, including the right of reproduction in whole or in part in any form. LITTLE SIMON is a registered trademark of Simon & Schuster, LLC, and associated colophon is a trademark of Simon & Schuster, LLC.
For information about special discounts for bulk purchases, please contact Simon & Schuster Special Sales at 1-866-506-1949 or business@simonandschuster.com. The Simon & Schuster Speakers Bureau can bring authors to your live event. For more information or to book an event contact the Simon & Schuster Speakers Bureau at 1-866-248-3049 or visit our website at www.simonspeakers.com.
Designed by Chrisila Maida
Manufactured in the United States of America 1123 LAK
10 9 8 7 6 5 4 3 2 1
Library of Congress Cataloging-in-Publication Data
Names: Coven, Wanda, author. | Burris, Priscilla, illustrator. | Title: Henry Heckelbeck makes super slime / by Wanda Coven ; illustrated by Priscilla Burris. | Description: First Little Simon paperback edition. | New York : Little Simon, 2023. | Series: Henry Heckelbeck ; book 14 | Audience: Ages 5–9. | Summary: To avert disaster, Henry must find a way to stop his super slime from swallowing everything in its path. | Identifiers: LCCN 2023028061 (print) | LCCN 2023028062 (ebook) | ISBN 9781665952842 (paperback) | ISBN 9781665952859 (hardcover) | ISBN 9781665952866 (ebook) | Subjects: CYAC: Magic—Fiction. | Slime (Toys)—Fiction. | Friendship—Fiction. | Classification: LCC PZ7.C83393 Hqm 2023 (print) | LCC PZ7.C83393 (ebook) | DDC [Fic]—dc23 | LC record available at https://lccn.loc.gov/2023028061 | LC ebook record available at https://lccn.loc.gov/2023028062

CONTENTS

Chapter 1 DR. BOT 1

Chapter 2 ONCE UPON A SLIME 9

Chapter 3 DIY SLIME 19

Chapter 4 SLIME BUCKET 33

Chapter 5 AS SLIME GOES BY 43

Chapter 6 GLURP! GLORP! 57

Chapter 7 HOW SLIME FLIES 69

Chapter 8 SLIME AND PUNISHMENT 81

Chapter 9 THE GOO CREW 91

Chapter 10 LEVEL ONE HUNDRED 107

Chapter 1

DR. BOT

"Guess WHAT?" shouted Henry Heckelbeck.

"Chicken butt!" yelled Dudley Day as he zipped down the slide. To Henry, it sounded like this: "Chicken BUUUTT!"

Henry laughed and pulled a cube from his pocket. He fiddled with it until it unfolded into a robot. "Meet Dr. Bot! It's a robot, puzzle, and action figure . . . all in one!"

Henry pushed a button on the back of his robot. *Zeedle zeedle! Zirrrrip!* it chirped.

Then Henry pushed another button. *Zeeep! Zeeeeep!* Red laser beams shot from the robot's eyes.

Max Maplethorpe zipped down the slide too. "Let ME see!" she said.

Dudley pushed the buttons and twisted the robot into different poses. "That's the coolest thing I've seen all day!" he said.

"Look!" Max said, pointing toward the swings. "There's a bunch of kids over there."

"Let's go see what's up," said Dudley, handing Dr. Bot back to Henry. Then Dudley and Max ran over to the crowd.

What could possibly be cooler than my new toy? Henry wondered. He folded up his robot and ran after his friends. He needed to find out!

Chapter 2

ONCE UPON A SLIME

All the kids were crowded around Sarah Sanchez. She had sparkly, neon slime in her hands. She stretched it like a giant glob of taffy. Then she smooshed it back together.

"It even glows in the dark!"
Sarah said, passing around
her slime.

The kids took turns jabbing
their fingers into it. "It's so soft
and flubbery!"

Dudley let out a giggle as he stretched the slime every which way.

Max squished the slime with both hands. It oozed between her fingers. "Totally flubberistic!" She passed the slime to Henry.

Henry passed it on without a single squish. He didn't want to seem interested, because he *wasn't*.

What's the big deal? Henry thought. *Slime isn't that cool. My robot is WAY cooler.*

Henry pressed Dr. Bot's buttons, but nobody noticed the robotic beeps and laser beams. The ooey, gooey slime had taken over everyone's attention.

"This slime is the most AMAZING thing ever!" said Aida Ackers.

Henry rolled his eyes. "It's just SLIME," he said. "Anyone can make slime."

Sarah narrowed her eyes. "No way! This is LEVEL SEVEN slime. It's really hard to make."

Henry's face flushed. "I make level seven slime all the time," he replied, but he wasn't sure if this was true.

He had made slime before with his sister, Heidi. He didn't know if it was really "level seven slime," or not, though.

Sarah folded her arms. "If you've made level seven slime, then why don't you bring it tomorrow?"

Henry gulped. "Sure!" he said, trying to sound confident. "Tomorrow I'll bring the best level seven slime ever!"

The kids all cheered. And suddenly Henry's insides felt like a big glob of twisty, knotted *slime*.

Chapter 3

DIY SLIME

When Henry got home, the living room table was covered with art supplies.

"I'm having an arts-and-crafts party today," Heidi said. "The theme is Sweet Treats."

Henry followed his sister into the kitchen. "Sounds fun," he said. "Can I borrow your book of slime recipes?"

Heidi whirled around. "Don't even THINK about going into my room!" she warned.

Henry held up his hands. "I promise I wasn't thinking about it! But will you get the book for me? I want to do arts-and-crafts too."

"You'll have to wait," Heidi answered. "I'm busy getting ready for my party."

Henry sat down. "How LONG will THAT take?"

Heidi didn't answer. Instead, she started scooping balls of cookie dough onto cookie sheets. Mom placed them in the oven. Then Heidi and Mom squeezed lemons to make lemonade.

Henry let out a yawn. "Can you squeeze any FASTER?" he asked.

"I'll be finished faster if you help," Heidi shot back.

Henry hopped off the stool and went to the pantry. He came back with a stack of green plates and a tower of yellow cups.

"Thanks!" Heidi said. She arranged the freshly baked cookies on the platter, one by one. Henry drummed his fingers on the counter and waited.

Henry knew the party was just for three people: Heidi and her two best friends, Lucy Lancaster and Bruce Bickerson. So why did it take so long to get ready?

Heidi finished arranging the cookies. She wiped her hands together. "Okay, now we can get the book."

Finally! Henry bolted from the kitchen and bounded up the stairs. He waited outside Heidi's bedroom door. It had a sign on it.

KEEP OUT!

Heidi caught up and opened the door. Henry raced to the bookshelf and yanked out the slime book. It was called *DIY: Do-It-Yourself Slime.*

"Will you make slime with me?" Henry asked. "I've never made it by myself."

"Not now. Bruce and Lucy are coming over," Heidi said. She ushered Henry out of her room.

"Just follow the directions. It's easy!" Heidi said, closing her door.

Henry sighed. Following directions was not exactly his greatest strength.

Chapter 4

SLIME BUCKET

Henry went to his room and flipped through the pages of the slime book. But he didn't find a single recipe for level seven slime. The book only went to level five!

If I don't make level seven, then my NAME will be SLIME! Henry thought. *Maybe I can buy some slime at the store and put it into another container.*

Then he shook his head. *What if I got CAUGHT?*

Henry flipped to one of the level five recipes. *What if I add extra ingredients to this recipe?* he wondered. *That might take the slime up to a level seven!*

Henry got right to work. He gathered the ingredients and laid them out on his desk.

Then he measured the ingredients into the bowl and stirred with a spoon.

But no matter how much he stirred, the mix didn't turn into soft, stretchy slime. It looked more like lumpy white glop.

"I know! It needs food coloring!" Henry said.

He raced to the pantry and grabbed blue food coloring. Seven drops went into his level seven slime. *Plip! Plop! Plip! Plop! Plip! Plop! Plip!*

Henry swirled in the food
coloring. The mix became
bright blue, but it still didn't
feel like slime. It was just
lumpy *blue* glop.

"I'm doomed!" Henry wailed,
moping back to his room.

He flung himself onto his
bed and closed his eyes.

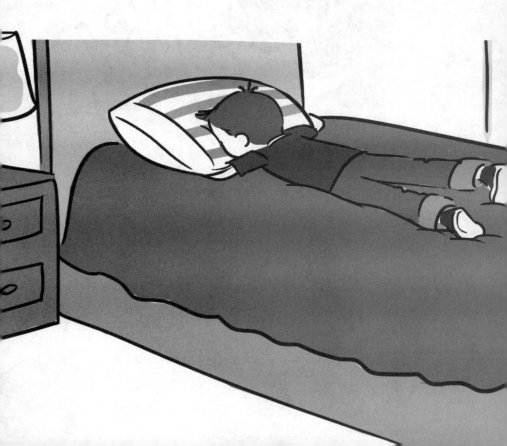

Now everyone's going to laugh and call me a big fat LIAR! he thought. *Or worse, a big fat SLIME BUCKET!*

Chapter 5

AS SLIME GOES BY

Henry heard a noise. He opened his eyes and sat up. "My magic book!" he shouted.

Henry's magic book floated down from the bookshelf and landed on his lap.

Pop! The medallion snapped free from the cover and came to rest around his neck.

The book opened, and the pages began to turn by themselves. They fluttered to a stop on a spell.

The Perfect Slime

Do your slime recipes turn out too sticky, too goopy, or too gloppy? Have you always wanted to make the kind of slime that's the envy of everyone on the playground? If you want to make the perfect silky slime, then this is the spell for you!

Ingredients:
12 marshmallows
1 jar of fruit jelly
2 rubber bands

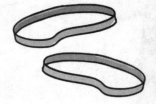

Start with a clean space. Place the ingredients in a bowl. Hold your medallion in one hand and place the other over the mix. Chant the following spell:

It's squishy, squashy, mooshy, gooshy, ooey, gooey TIME! Turn my goopy, gloppy words into perfect SLIME!

Warning: Loud noises will frighten the slime back into its original state.

Henry gathered the spell ingredients and placed them in a clean bowl. He was so excited to cast his spell that he forgot to first tidy his desk.

Henry held his medallion in his right hand and placed his left hand over the mix. He chanted the spell.

A cloud of glittery magic swirled around everything on his desk—including the lumpy slime, the mixing spoon, and Dr. Bot.

Suddenly Dr. Bot began to unfold all by itself!

"My robot is alive!" Henry shouted. He watched Dr. Bot pick up the spoon.

After a few seconds the toy dropped the spoon, folded back into a cube, and fell on its side.

Henry picked up his robot and pressed the buttons. *Zeeep! Zeeeeep!* Dr. Bot was back to behaving like usual.

A new batch of
slime sat inside
the bowl. It was
smooth, shiny,
and slimy.

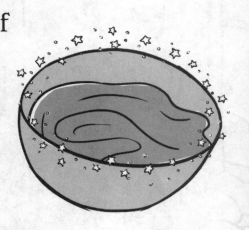

   "I did it!" Henry said,
doing a little victory dance.

He looked back in the bowl. Only this time, he thought he saw the slime *move*. He rubbed his eyes. *Slime can't move by itself!* he thought. *That's just my imagination.*

But Henry's imagination wasn't playing tricks on him. The slime *was* moving . . . and it was slowly creeping up and out of the bowl!

Chapter 6

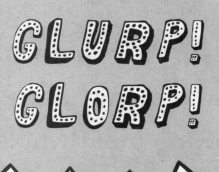

GLURP! GLORP!

"Creepy crawlers! My SLIME is alive too!" Henry shouted.

The slime slithered onto the desk. It oozed over Dr. Bot. The toy disappeared into the middle of the mushy, gushy slime.

Then the slime glopped onto the floor. *Plop!* It stretched over Henry's magnifying glass and one of his dirty socks, swallowing them whole.

"Hey! Those are mine!" Henry said.

The slime paid no attention to Henry and slithered on.

"STOP!" Henry lunged for the slime and grabbed it with both hands. But the slime slipped through his hands like a wet bar of soap. *Glurp!*

The slime oozed out of Henry's room and into the hallway. It picked up speed and flip-flopped down the stairs. *Gloink! Glunk! Gloink!* Henry raced after the slime.

It oozed by Heidi's party in the living room. Luckily, no one noticed as Henry tiptoed by and ran into the kitchen.

The slime had just finished raiding the fridge. It belched, then crawled onto the counter and knocked over a bag of flour.

Clunk! POOF! The bag burst open on the floor, and a big cloud of flour rose into the air. Henry began to cough like crazy.

"Is that you, Henry?" Heidi called from the living room.

Henry wiped the flour from his face. "Yup! I'm definitely—*cough, cough*—ALONE!"

But, of course, Henry was *not* alone. The slime was now reaching toward Heidi's cookie platter.

Henry dove for the platter and pulled it away from the very hungry slime.

Heidi will kill me if anything happens to the cookies! he thought, holding the platter tightly.

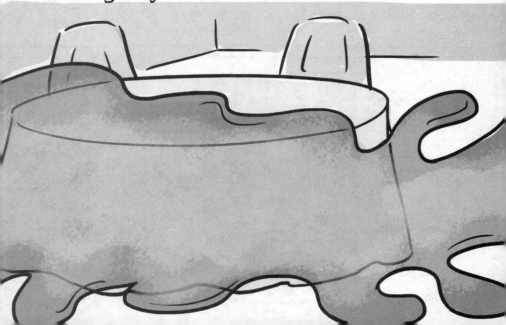

Henry turned to close the fridge door. That's when he spied an empty container of chocolate milk on the floor.

Oh no! thought Henry. *What if the slime also drank Heidi's lemonade?*

Chapter 7

HOW SLIME FLIES

After opening the fridge, Henry sighed with relief. The lemonade jug was still inside.

Henry entered spy mode, checking the fridge to see if anything else was missing.

He spied an empty pizza box.

He also spied two empty food containers.

If I had my magnifying glass, I could detect what had been inside these containers! he thought. Then he remembered the slime had eaten his magnifying glass.

And speaking of slime . . . where was it now?

Henry turned around and jumped. The slime was right behind him, chomping on one of Heidi's cookies! Henry looked at the nearly empty platter and then looked back at the slime.

They both gulped. "BAD
SLIME!" Henry whispered.

The slime quivered and
quaked. Its body began to
bulge. Then it bounced on
the floor like an overgrown
bouncy ball.

Boing! *Squelch!* *Boing!* *Squash!* The slime bounced off the ceiling, the cupboards, and the counters.

It splattered onto the kitchen table and then to the oven. The slime had gone bonkers!

It gulped down water from the faucet. *Glug! Glug! Glug!* The slime grew even bigger, like a massive water balloon.

Henry bolted to the sink and shut off the water.

Oh no! What if the slime eats the entire kitchen? he thought. *What if it eats the whole neighborhood?*

What if it takes over the whole WORLD?

Henry had to do something to stop the slime . . . *now*!

Chapter 8

SLIME AND PUNISHMENT

Henry took a deep breath and prepared to battle the slime. Some leftover flour dust tickled his nose. *"AH-CHOO!"*

The slime stopped chewing a dish towel.

Henry sneezed again. *"Ah, ah, AH-CHOOOOOO!"*

The slime froze. That's when Henry remembered the spell had said loud noises would *reverse* the magic.

Henry thought of an idea. He grabbed the last cookie from the platter and waved it at the slime.

"Here, slimy, slimy!"

The slime launched toward the cookie and swallowed it, along with Henry's arm. Henry reached around deep inside the slime. He felt his sock and magnifying glass.

Henry reached farther until he found his robot toy. He grabbed Dr. Bot and began to push its buttons.

Zeeep! Zeeeeep! Zeedle zeedle! Zirrrrip!

The slime jiggled and shook violently. *KA-SPLOOOOSH!* The great blob of slime collapsed into a puddle of blue goo.

Henry stared at the glop on his hands and the puddle on the floor. He waited a few moments, but it didn't move a muscle.

Just then he heard footsteps approaching the kitchen.

"My mom and I made the BEST lemonade and cookies!" Heidi said to her friends Lucy Lancaster and Bruce Bickerson as they entered the kitchen.

Then they saw the mess.

"Henry?" cried Heidi. She noticed the empty cookie platter. "What happened to my cookies?!"

Chapter 9

THE GOO CREW

"Sorry, Heidi," Henry said, looking down at his feet. "The lemonade is still in the fridge."

Bruce pointed to the slime gunk in Henry's hand. "Is that taffy or something?"

Henry shook his head sadly.
"It was slime, but it didn't turn
out right."

Lucy poked the slimy bits.

"Are those cookie crumbs inside?" she asked.

"Yup, the slime was hungry," said Henry.

Both Lucy and Bruce laughed, but Heidi put her hands on her hips. "Henry, if you wanted to join our party, then why didn't you say so? You didn't have to make a mess in the kitchen to get our attention."

Henry frowned. That wasn't the reason the kitchen was a mess, but he wasn't about to say *magic* had caused the disaster.

"We can help you make better slime," Heidi continued.

"But first we have to clean up the kitchen before Mom comes downstairs. Or else we'll all get into huge trouble!"

Everyone helped clean the kitchen. Then they poured themselves lemonade and went to the living room.

Heidi, Bruce, and Lucy helped Henry make a new batch of slime. When it was finished, Henry sank his hands into the slippery, shiny slime.

"That sure is level five slime!" Heidi said, poking it.

"But level five isn't enough," Henry said. He had told Sarah that he would bring level seven slime.

Henry looked at the art supplies on the table. There were things like pom-poms for making ice-cream cones and cupcake-shaped beads for making bracelets.

Then Henry added a few secret ingredients to his slime. "Ta-da!" he announced. "I am introducing the all-new-and-improved slime!"

Heidi and her friends gathered to take a look.

"Wowza!" Bruce shouted, clapping his hands.

"I've never seen anything like it!" Lucy added.

Henry smiled proudly. "Just call me Dr. Slime!"

Chapter 10

LEVEL ONE HUNDRED

"What's inside that plastic container?" asked Max at the playground the next day.

Henry wiggled his eyebrows. "Nothing much. Just my . . . SUPERSLIME!"

Henry popped the lid from
the container, and his friends
peeked inside.

The silver glitter, which Henry had mixed in as a secret ingredient, sparkled in the sun.

"It's shiny, like metal!" cried Dudley.

Max used both hands to squeeze the slime. "It's sooo super squooshy!"

Henry pulled out two googly eyes from his pocket and took back the slime. "Wait till you see the best part."

He pushed the googly eyes into the slime so it had a face. Then he held it up. "Now it's ROBOT slime! *Beep! Bop! I. Am. A. ROBOT.* Prepare for a robot invasion!"

Max and Dudley squealed and took off running. Henry charged after them with his robot slime. When they ran out of breath, the friends fell over, laughing.

Sarah walked up to them. "Did you bring your slime, Henry?"

Henry gave her the slime.

Sarah poked it and gave it back. "That's NOT level seven slime," she said.

Henry's stomach tightened. "Well, that's because it's my own special recipe," he answered.

Max folded her arms. "That's right!" she said. "It's level ONE HUNDRED slime!"

"Whatever," Sarah huffed, and she walked away.

The three best friends slapped each other high-fives.

"So, are you going to make level one thousand slime tomorrow?" asked Dudley.

Henry shook his head. "Trust me, you don't ever want to see level one thousand slime. It's so powerful, it could eat up all of Brewster!"

Max's eyes widened. "If anyone could do it, it would be you!"

Henry laughed. "Yeah, and you know what I'd call it?"

He raised his arms like a monster. "FRANKEN-SLIME!"

Max and Dudley screamed, and Henry chased them all over again.

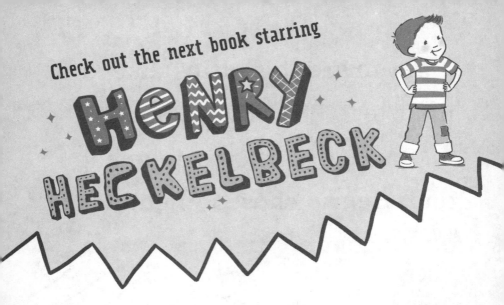

Check out the next book starring

HENRY HECKELBECK

Henry loved Saturday lunches. On Saturdays he got to have dinosaur chicken nuggets and applesauce.

Henry glanced at the kitchen calendar.

An excerpt from *Henry Heckelbeck Does Not Need a Sitter*

Today's date had a big red heart on it. *That's weird,* he thought. *It's not even Valentine's Day!*

"Why is there a heart drawn on today's date?" Henry asked his mom and dad, who were also eating lunch at the kitchen table.

His parents looked at each other. Then they kissed.

Henry covered his eyes.

An excerpt from *Henry Heckelbeck Does Not Need a Sitter*

GROSS! he thought.

"Today is our anniversary!" said Dad.

Henry peeked between his fingers. "What's *that*?"

"An anniversary remembers a special event from the past," said Mom. "We got married on this day many years ago."

An excerpt from *Henry Heckelbeck Does Not Need a Sitter*